Kribit
The Red Toad from
Maryland

By Lisa Downey Merriam

Red Toad Press, New York, NY

Copyright © 2008 by Lisa Downey Merriam.
Printed in the United States of America

This is a work of fiction. Names, characters, places an incidents either are the product of
the author's imagination or are used fictitiously. Any resemblance to any actual persons,
living ro dead, events, or locales is entirely coincidental.

ISBN-13: 978-0-9820829-0-4

10 9 8 7 6 5 4 3 2

For Lucy and Joe
with much love

When I was little, I used to visit Uncle Lawrence's farm in the rolling hills along the Potomac River in Washington County, Maryland.

Uncle Lawrence lived in an old stone house up on a bluff overlooking the river.

I liked to hike up to the sheep pasture where an enormous tree had branches that hung all the way to the ground. I liked to swing from the vines hanging from the branches, my feet brushing the wooly backs of the sheep.

No matter how hot the day, the shade of that tree was cool and inviting.

I would swing under the tree until my Aunt Pauline rang the farm bell for lunch.

I walked along the cow path down the hill back to the house, dragging a stick and kicking at the clods of red dirt.

Suddenly my eye was drawn to one clod of dirt that kept moving. I looked again and the dirt clod jumped. It was hopping!

It wasn't a dirt clod at all. It was a toad--a tiny toad, as red as the Maryland dirt.

I sprung into action and caught him in my hands. He was the most beautiful creature, all red and warty, with golden eyes. He was only the size of a quarter.

I ran down the hill and called for Uncle Lawrence. He lit up with excitement over the tiny toad.

He took me to the icehouse and found a big empty pickle jar. We put the toad inside so we could examine him in detail. He was beautiful!

My Uncle Lawrence said he was the finest looking toad he had ever seen and asked me if I had a name for him.

I thought for a moment and named him Kribit.

"Kribit needs more than a glass jar to be happy," he said.

We put some dirt and weeds in the bottom of the jar and placed a little bowl of water inside.

"Now that's a terrarium," said Uncle Lawrence. "Kribit will feel more at home if he can sit on some nice, red Maryland dirt and hide under some leaves."

Uncle Lawrence thought Kribit might be hungry. We put some peanut butter out on a plate in the garden.

"Toads like to eat ants," said Uncle Lawrence. "Let's see what we can catch."

In a half hour, we had many, many, many juicy ants.

Indeed Kribit was hungry. When he heard the ants, he became very alert. He began to slowly creep up on them. When he got close, he froze. Quicker than I could see, Kribit's tongue shot out and one ant disappeared into his mouth.

"Can I keep him?" I asked.

Uncle Lawrence said that Kribit would be happier on the farm, but seeing how much I loved him, I could take him home to Chicago. He made me promise the minute I failed to take good care of the toad, I had to bring him back to the farm.

I carried Kribit in his pickle jar very carefully onto the plane and showed him off to the pilot.

I held Kribit's jar in my lap. The pilot announced to everyone that he would try to make the flight extra smooth because of our unusual little passenger.

When I got home, my mother helped me make a terrarium--something bigger than the pickle jar. When everything was ready, we put Kribit inside. My mother put a screen over the top and attached it with a rubber band so Kribit could not get out.

In the middle of the night, a strange sound awakened me. I got a flashlight out of my nightstand and followed the sound. It was coming from Kribit's terrarium.

I flashed my light around and there he was. Kribit's throat was blown up like a bubble. He was singing a toad song. It sounded a little sad.

Everything went well for a while. I fed Kribit every day. Every night he sang me to sleep.

When school started, I got very busy. I thought about Kribit less and less. My mother had to remind me to feed him.

One day, I forgot to put the lid on his terrarium and I forgot to feed him. Days passed before I thought of him. I went to check on him and discovered he was gone! The terrarium was empty! No Kribit!

I looked everywhere and finally found him hidden on the second floor of my doll house, looking sad and hungry.

My mother said a doll house was no place for a toad. Kribit had to return to Maryland.

27

When Spring came, I put Kribit in the pickle jar and flew back to Maryland.

Uncle Lawrence and I carried Kribit to the exact place where I first found him. I picked him out of the jar and gave him a last kiss. Then I set him down on the red Maryland dirt.

Kribit looked around nervously and hopped to the edge of the lane. Then he disappeared under some leaves. He was home.

I was sad watching Kribit hop away, but I knew my mother was right. He did not belong in a doll house or a terrarium. He belonged on a farm in Maryland. There he could sing--not sad songs to a little girl-- but happy ones to other toads.

I like to think Kribit lived a long and happy life and that his children and grandchildren still hop along the red dirt country lanes on my Uncle Lawrence's farm.

And if toads could talk, he certainly would have an unusual tale to tell his friends. How many toads fly in jets?

31

Red Toad
press

Copies of *Kribit the Red Toad from Maryland* can be
purchased at all major booksellers and directly from
www.redtoadpress.com

CPSIA information can be obtained
at www.ICGtesting.com
Printed in the USA
BVHW022153180820
586773BV00008B/43